It All Began with a Bean

by

Katie McKy

Illustrated by Tracy Hill

Tanglewood Press • Terre Haute, IN

Published by Tanglewood Press, LLC, November 2004.

Book and text design by Amy Alick Perich.

Tanglewood Press, LLC
P. O. Box 3009
Terre Haute, IN 47803
www.tanglewoodbooks.com

Printed in the United States of America

10 9 8 7 6 5 4 3 2 1

ISBN 0-9749303-0-X

All animals and people fart. Many things can make a fart.

Beans can make a fart. So can raisins, cheese, potato chips, gum, eggs, and soda.

Even swallowing too much air can make a fart!

And this is the true story of what happened when everything and everyone farted at once.

It all began with a bean.

That bean fell from a boy's burrito.

Now, a bean is a FEAST for flies, so five flies came and fed on that bean.

Then off they flew.

Then it got worse. A girl in a park spilled her whole big box of raisins. Fifteen pigeons flew to those raisins and ate them faster than that girl could give a quick cry. Then the fifteen pigeons flew off.

Then forty-five cats happened to ask for "Cheese, please." Although it just sounded like "Meow, meow," their owners understood.

Then a chip truck hit a bump, and all the bags bounced out the back.

One hundred and thirty-five dogs got rich whiffs of those potato chips. They jumped out windows, burrowed under fences, left Frisbees in flight, and sprinted after the truck.

They ate and ate and ate—all of the chips!—and only then did all those dogs go back to where they belonged.

Just then the teachers at the elementary schools, for a final-day treat, passed out bubble gum. Thousands and thousands of kids chewed. Teachers chewed, too.

Then more than half a million people decided to cook the very same thing—eggs! Some were scrambled, some were hardboiled, and some were sunny-side up, but they were all eggs: hundreds of thousands of them.

And every one was eaten.

Then a soft drink factory, high on a hill, had a big spill. The kids were all in school, unlucky for them. So the soda rushed right into the Blue River, where it seemed safe. But a million fish swam through it.

Then it got as bad as it could be. A race was about to begin. The runners jogged in place, taking big breaths.

Millions of people cheered, taking bigger breaths.

The woman with the starter's pistol pulled the trigger.
BANG!
And that's when it happened.

The flies and the pigeons and the cats and the dogs farted.
The students farted...and the teachers, too.
Half a million people washing their egg dishes farted.
A million fish in the river farted.
Millions of people cheering for the runners farted.
They all farted at once!

For half a second, everything seemed fine. Dogs jumped a little higher.
Pigeons popped off statues.

The runners finished the race in record time...although no one was left to cheer their finish!

And then, oh, can you guess what happened?

The blast of the gas blew the paint from police cars to school buses.
And vice versa.

Saddles were blown off horses' backs and onto the backs of cowboys.
Grandmas were blown out of rocking chairs and onto skateboards.

Kids on swing sets were blown all the way around–three times.
The blast blew the stripes off zebras, and onto zookeepers.
But the zebras didn't have to walk around in bright white for long.
Patterns were blown off dresses and onto zebras.

The gas parted the threads in teachers' clothes.
The kids got to see the principal's underpants!
The high hills on the roller coaster shriveled, which wasn't much fun for kids,
but it was a fine new ride for their grandparents.

Fish from the river were carried high in bubbles of gas,
which happened to pass over swimming pools, and that's
where they popped…

…which made for strange swimming, but…

…fine fishing.

And then the blast passed, but…
…not the smell.

And oh, that smell! It was so strong that green slid out of the leaves of trees.

Freckles slid off cheeks.
The curls on poodles went long and limp.
Bald eagles became BALD eagles.

The stink was so stinky that the Pork Farm's pigs corked their snouts.
Elephants plugged their trunks with bananas.

Looking like ostriches, the ladies of the
Gardening Club stuck their heads in flowerbeds.

Even skunks searching for food in trashcans had to close their noses.
Stores sold clothespins for ten dollars apiece. And they sold every single one.

Luckily, late that afternoon, there was a mighty wind that came through and blew the gas away. So life was good again.

Except for those downwind of that town.